Saying Goodbye to Lulu

by CORINNE DEMAS   Illustrated by ARD HOYT

LITTLE, BROWN AND COMPANY
New York Boston

Little, Brown and Company

Hachette Book Group
1290 Avenue of the Americas, New York, NY 10104
Visit our Web site at www.lb-kids.com

Little, Brown and Company is a division of Hachette Book Group, Inc.
The Little, Brown name and logo are trademarks of Hachette Book Group, Inc.

The publisher is not responsible for websites (or their content) that are not owned by the publisher.

First Paperback Edition: September 2009
Originally published in hardcover in 2004 by Little, Brown and Company

Library of Congress Cataloging-in-Publication Data

Demas, Corinne.
   Saying Goodbye to Lulu / by Corinne Demas; illustrated by Ard Hoyt.
      p. cm.
   Summary: When her dog Lulu dies, a girl grieves but then continues with her life.
   ISBN 978-0-316-70278-2 (HC) / ISBN 978-0-316-04749-4 (PB)
      [1. Death — Fiction. 2. Dogs — Fiction. 3. Pets — Fiction. 4. Grief — Fiction.] I. Hoyt, Ard, ill. II. Title.

PZ7.D39145Say2004
[E] — dc21   2003044690

10

APS

Manufactured in China

The illustrations for this book were done in watercolor, colored pencil, and pen and ink on Arches paper.
The text was set in Fairfield LH Medium, and the display type is BigBlueDot and Erazure.

For my agent and friend, Tracey Adams
—C.D.

To Steven Kellogg,
who loves dogs and inspired me
—A.H.

When my dog Lulu got really old
she couldn't climb the stairs anymore.
She'd wait for me at the bottom
and her tail would go *thump, thump*.
Sometimes she didn't hear me calling her,
and when we went on walks she stayed close beside me
because she couldn't see well.

When Lulu couldn't walk anymore
I would carry her out to the grass.
When she couldn't see or hear at all, she could still smell.
She would lift her head to sniff the outside world.

I fed her from my hand and held her water bowl
so she could drink.

I put all her dog toys—her squeaky and her rawhide chew and my old slipper—nearby her.

At night I covered her with my blue sweater, the one she always pulled off my chair and curled up with when I wasn't home.

"Sweetheart, you can't make her well again," Mommy said at dinnertime.

I kicked the leg of the table. "I know that," I said.

I lay down beside Lulu and stroked her back.
Her fur was soft and fuzzy, but underneath
I could feel her bones.
She licked my hand. She could still lick.

"I love you, Lulu," I said.
But she already knew that.

"We'll get another dog after Lulu,"
Daddy said.

"I don't want another dog. I want Lulu back,
the way she used to be," I said.

I wanted Lulu to come dashing out to meet my bus
when I came home from school.

I wanted Lulu to play catch with my old ball
and bring it back, even when I threw it as far as I could throw.

I wanted Lulu to go mucking in the stream with me
and climbing on the rocks with me
and exploring in the woods with me.

I wanted Lulu to race me up the stairs to bed
and bark until Daddy came to read us our goodnight story.

One day, Lulu couldn't stand up. She slept all day.
She didn't eat. She wet her bed.
"It's like when she was a newborn puppy,"
Mommy said.
That was before I was born.

"What was she like then?" I asked.
"Her eyes weren't open and she couldn't see,
    she couldn't stand up, and she didn't eat real food yet.
    She slept all the time," said Mommy.

When I came home from school the next day,
Mommy told me Lulu was dead.
She took me on her lap and we both cried.
"Do you want to see her and say goodbye?" Mommy asked.
I wanted to say goodbye, but I was afraid, too.

Mommy held me close.

It was Lulu's body, but so still,

still as the floor or the walls or the chair.

Mommy reached out and ran her hand along Lulu's back.

She held my hand so I could touch Lulu's fur.

It was soft and fuzzy.

I wanted to say goodbye to Lulu,

but all I could do was cry.

We put Lulu in a box with her favorite toys
and a sock from each of us that smelled like us.
We covered her with my blue sweater.
We buried the box in the backyard.
"We'll have to wait till spring to plant something here,"
said Mommy.
But I already knew that.

I put a stone with sparkly bits of mica in it to mark the place.
I wanted to say goodbye to Lulu,
but all I could do was cry instead.

I missed Lulu every day.
I missed the sound of her tail going *thump, thump*
while she waited for me at the bottom of the stairs,
and the smell of her when she licked my hand,
and the feel of her soft fur.

When springtime came we planted
a cherry tree with pink flowers by her grave.
Lulu's tree, I called it.
I knelt in its small circle of shade.
I stroked the new, fresh-green grass.
"Goodbye, Lulu," I said, softly.

Now it is almost Summer.
We're getting a new puppy
when he is old enough to leave his mother.
I go to visit him. His eyes are closed and he can't see.
He can't stand and he can't eat real food yet.

I hold him in my arms.

He sniffs my hand and then he falls asleep.

I stroke his soft fur.

When he's bigger we'll play together under Lulu's tree.

"You're not Lulu," I whisper to him.
"Still, I'll love you, too."
But I think he already knows that.